The Winter's Tale

Sweet Cherry
Publishing

Published by Sweet Cherry Publishing Limited
Unit E, Vulcan Business Complex,
Vulcan Road,
Leicester, LE5 3EB,
United Kingdom

First published in the USA in 2013
ISBN: 978-1-78226-065-3

©Macaw Books

Title: The Winter's Tale
North American Edition

Text & Illustration by Macaw Books 2013

www.sweetcherrypublishing.com

Printed and bound by Wai Man Book Binding (China) Ltd. Kowloon, H.K.

About Shakespeare

William Shakespeare, regarded as the greatest writer in the English language, was born in Stratford-upon-Avon in Warwickshire, England (around April 23, 1564). He was the third of eight children born to John and Mary Shakespeare.

Shakespeare was a poet, playwright, and dramatist. He is often known as England's national poet and the "Bard of Avon." Thirty-eight plays, 154 sonnets, two long narrative poems, and several other poems are attributed to him. Shakespeare's plays have been translated into every major existent language and are performed more often than those of any other playwright.

Hermione: She is the beautiful and faithful wife of King Leontes. She is wrongly accused by her husband of being unfaithful. She dies of grief in the play but is restored to life at the end.

Polixenes: He is the King of Bohemia and childhood friend of Leontes. He is wrongfully accused

of having an affair with Hermione, Leontes's wife. He somehow manages to escape Sicily when Leontes plots to kill him.

Leontes: He is the King of Sicily. He has jealous fantasies and is convinced that his wife, Hermione, is having an affair with his childhood friend, Polixenes, who is the King of Bohemia. He acts cruelly toward his wife and later repents of his actions.

Shepherd: He is an old man and a good-natured, honorable shepherd. He raises Perdita, whom he finds as a baby, as his own daughter.

The Winter's Tale

Once upon a time, Sicily was ruled by a wise and able king called Leontes. He had a very beautiful and virtuous wife by the name of Hermione. Hermione was such

a gentle and loving wife that Leontes hardly had any reason for complaint. She took care of his every need, but there was one thing that was missing in his life—a reunion with his old childhood friend Polixenes, who was now the King of Bohemia.

They had been very close
friends from birth, but after the
deaths of their fathers, the boys
had become deeply involved
with their respective kingdoms
and, in time, lost touch. After
many requests and messages sent,
Polixenes agreed to visit Sicily
all the way from Bohemia.

Leontes was overjoyed to see his dear old friend again after such a long time. He introduced him to Hermione and the three of them would spend long hours chatting with one another, the two old friends recounting tales of their youth to the gentle Hermione.

Soon it was time for Polixenes to return to his kingdom.

Hermione joined her husband
in entreating their honored
guest to stay a little while longer.
However, this is when the
problems started. Polixenes
turned down the offer of staying
when his own dear friend Leontes

begged him, but when Hermione
asked him for the same favor, he
agreed to her proposal at once.

Leontes was suddenly
overcome by a spate of jealousy.
He did not know how he should

feel about what was happening. On top of that, Hermione's attention toward Polixenes, which she was continuing to give on the request of her husband, did not go down well with Leontes.

After this had gone on for some time, Leontes became a changed man. Once a caring and loving husband and friend, he had turned into a savage monster. Unable to bear the pangs of jealousy that he now had to face, Leontes sent for one of his lords at court, a man called Camillo, and ordered him to poison Polixenes.

But Camillo was a good man and he knew that what his king had asked him to do was wrong. So, instead of poisoning Polixenes, he informed the King of Bohemia about the plan. Together, they planned to escape from Sicily. Thus, with the help of Camillo, Polixenes was able to return

to his kingdom of Bohemia
safely. He then appointed
Camillo at his court, and soon
Camillo became the king's
best friend and chief adviser.

Back in Sicily, Polixenes's
flight had greater repercussions

than anyone could have
imagined. Infuriated that the
villain who had tried to woo his
wife was still safe and sound,
Leontes decided to take up
the matter with Hermione.
He stormed into her chambers
and, sending their son,

Mamillius, away, immediately
imprisoned his own wife.

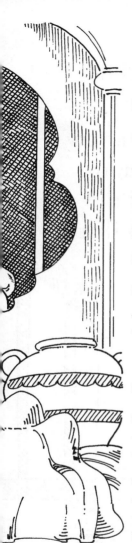

Mamillius was very fond of his mother and could not bear to see her dishonored in this way. He was so grief-stricken that he stopped eating and soon it seemed that the young prince might die.

Meanwhile, Leontes sent two of his lords at court, Cleomenes and Dion, to the Oracle of Apollo, and asked Delphos to find out if his wife had been unfaithful. Meanwhile, Hermione gave birth to a little girl, the newborn child her only comfort in prison.

Now, Hermione had a very good friend called Paulina, the wife of Lord Antigonus at the court of Leontes. Hearing that

Hermione had given birth to a baby girl, Paulina immediately rushed to the prison and asked Emilia, the lady who was taking care of Hermione and the baby, to tell the queen that she wanted

to have the baby given to her. She
declared that she would take the
baby to the father, and perhaps
the sight of the newborn child
would soften his heart. She also
told Emilia to inform the queen
that she would defend her in
the highest manner possible.

Paulina, with the little baby in her arms, forced her way into the court. Her husband tried to stop her, fearing that this would only enrage the king, but Paulina would not listen to anyone. Presenting

herself before the
king, she placed the
little baby at his
feet. She went on
to tell him how he
had wrongly imprisoned his
devoted wife and begged him

to release her from prison.
But her entire demonstration
only served to anger the king
further, and he immediately
asked Antigonus to take his
wife away from the court.

The minute Paulina left,
Leontes called Antigonus
and asked him to take the
little baby and leave it in the
desert to perish. Antigonus
was no Camillo and did just
as his king had ordered. He
immediately took the baby

away, intending to leave her in the first desert he could find.

Leontes was now seething for reasons beyond anyone's understanding. He could not wait for his two lords to return from the Oracle and gave Hermione a public trial, wanting to issue her with a just punishment for her folly. When everyone had gathered around poor Hermione, who was now a prisoner before them, both Cleomenes and

Dion entered the court with the
Oracle's declaration.

It stated, "Hermione is innocent, Polixenes blameless—Camillo is a true subject, Leontes a jealous tyrant, and the king shall live without an heir if she who is lost be not found."

Leontes was so headstrong that he found the Oracle to be false and asked the jury present

to proceed with their judgment on the prisoner. Just at that moment, a man entered the assembly and declared that the young prince Mamillius, upon hearing that his mother was being tried for a crime she did not commit, had died of shock.

Hearing the news of the death of her son, Hermione

fainted. Leontes felt sorry for his wife and asked her attendants

to take her away and try to revive her. But Paulina soon returned to the assembly and informed the king that Hermione was indeed dead.

It was only then that Leontes repented his cruelty toward his wife. He knew that her heart was pure and she was indeed innocent. He also realized

that if his daughter were left
in the desert, then the Oracle
would be proved right and
he would be left heirless.

Meanwhile, as these
thoughts were going through

the king's mind, Antigonus,
after being caught in a storm,
had been redirected toward
Bohemia. He arrived on the
coast of Bohemia and carried out
the king's orders. Leaving the

baby there, he was about to turn
back and leave for Sicily when a
bear emerged from behind the
bushes and tore him apart.

A poor shepherd, walking
along the coast, came across
the baby. He saw that she was
dressed in rich clothes and

jewels, and a scrap of paper
was tied to her arm which
read "Perdita." Being a kind
man, the shepherd took the
baby with him. His wife was
overjoyed to see the baby. The

shepherd used the jewelry to
buy many sheep and goats,
and soon, he became very rich.
He raised Perdita as his own,
and she came to be known
as the shepherd's daughter.

Now, Polixenes
had a young son called
Florizel. One day, when
Florizel was walking in
the palace grounds, he
saw the beautiful Perdita
and immediately fell in
love with her. He did
not tell her that he was
a prince, but instead
introduced himself as
Doricles, a gentleman
who lived nearby.
They soon became
very good friends.

One day, Polixenes
sent some people to
follow Florizel, as he
wanted to know where

his son went every day. When
the men came back and told
the king what they had seen,
the king and Camillo decided
to pay the shepherd a visit,
dressed as mere travelers.

Festivities were being held
at the shepherd's house, and the
king and Camillo were warmly
welcomed. As they joined in with
the celebrations, they noticed
Florizel and Perdita sitting in a

corner. Rather than dancing and feasting, they sat quietly in each other's company. The king admitted that he had never seen a prettier girl in his life and Camillo could not help but comment, "Truly, she is the queen of curds and cream."

But then Polixenes revealed his true self and ordered his son never to see the

shepherd's daughter again,
or else he would have the
girl and her father killed.
As Polixenes left in a huff,
Camillo, who had been
enamored by Perdita's beauty,
asked the two lovers to leave
for Sicily and take shelter in
the court of King Leontes. So
Florizel, Perdita, and the old
shepherd made haste for Sicily.
The shepherd even took the
clothes and the note he had
found on the infant with him.

When the two love-struck
youths reached Leontes's court,
he welcomed them warmly. He
immediately developed a deep
affection for Perdita, whose

appearance reminded him of his own wife, Hermione. Looking at Perdita, he said, "Such a sweet creature my daughter might have been, if I had not cruelly sent her from me."

Hearing the king speak these words, the shepherd at once realized that Perdita was none other than the daughter Leontes

spoke of. He immediately
showed the king the clothes
and the piece of paper, and it

was ascertained that Perdita was indeed his long-lost daughter. The king was beside himself with joy and rewarded the shepherd handsomely for bringing his daughter back to him.

Polixenes, on learning that the girl he had forbidden his son from marrying was none other than the daughter of his dear friend, at once consented to the marriage. But even though everyone in the courts of both Sicily and Bohemia were very happy about the alliance, Leontes was sad when he remembered the harsh treatment he had meted out to his wife many years ago

and that Hermione could not
share with him this joyous day.

Paulina, who was now in
high favor with the king, came
over to Leontes and said that
she had created a lifelike statue
of Hermione, and now that

everything was fine again she
wanted to present it to him.
So Paulina, Florizel, Perdita,
and Leontes all set off toward
Paulina's house, where the
statue was shown to them.

Truly, never had there been a more life-like statue built of any person as the one that stood before them. While everyone present praised its beauty, Leontes remained silent; he could not bring himself to say anything. But after a while, he mentioned that unlike the statue, Hermione had few wrinkles on her face. Perdita interjected and said that perhaps the sculptor wanted to show them how she would look had she still been alive.

Paulina told the king that it
might be better if she drew the
curtains back over the statue,
as he seemed visibly pale. But
Leontes wanted to stare at the

statue for a while longer. Paulina
replied that if the king were to do
so, he might think it was alive.

At that moment, the statue
stepped off its pedestal and

walked up to the king, threw
her arms around him, and kissed
him. Hermione had not died
after all! She had been kept in
hiding by her faithful friend,
Paulina. And although she had

learned earlier that the king had repented his follies, she could not bring herself to show herself to him until she received news about her daughter. But now that Perdita had been found, she forgave her husband.

Perdita and Florizel were married, and in a way, it was like a second marriage for Leontes and Hermione. After all those years, Leontes was finally able to get the peace he so desperately wanted.